Clare Mackintosh is the author of *I Let You Go, I See You, Let Me Lie* and *After the End*. All of her books have been *Sunday Times* bestsellers and have sold more than 2 million copies worldwide. They have also been translated into over thirty-five languages.

Clare is patron of the Silver Star Society, a charity based at the John Radcliffe Hospital in Oxford, which supports parents facing high-risk or difficult pregnancies. She lives in North Wales with her husband and their three children.

For more information visit Clare's website www.claremackintosh.com or find her at www.facebook.com/ClareMackWrites or on Twitter @ClareMackint0sh

Also by Clare Mackintosh

I Let You Go
I See You
Let Me Lie
After the End

Non-fiction
A Cotswold Life

Clare Mackintosh

THE
DONOR

sphere

SPHERE

First published in Great Britain in 2020 by Sphere

5 7 9 10 8 6 4

A CIP catalogue record for this book
is available from the British Library.

ISBN 978-0-7515-7650-4

Typeset in Stone Serif by Palimpsest Book Production Limited,
Falkirk, Stirlingshire
Printed and bound in Great Britain by Clays Ltd, Elcograf S.p.A.

Papers used by Sphere are from well-managed forests
and other responsible sources.

Sphere
An imprint of
Little, Brown Book Group
Carmelite House
50 Victoria Embankment
London EC4Y 0DZ

An Hachette UK Company
www.hachette.co.uk

www.littlebrown.co.uk

Chapter 1

The Newspaper Article

The reporter is young, with too much gel in his hair, and a habit of saying 'wow, yeah, right,' after everything Meg says. She doesn't seem to notice, and has been happily chatting to him for half an hour.

'I had cancer when I was a toddler,' she tells him. 'I got better, but the treatment left me with a heart problem.' She shrugs, as if it was nothing, instead of an illness that has taken over our lives for the last twelve years. She is on the sofa in our living room, the reporter opposite her, on the armchair Steve sits on to watch the footy. I'm next to Meg, trying not to answer questions for her.

'Wow, yeah, right,' says the reporter, scribbling in his notebook. He's wearing a suit that looks as if he's borrowed it from his dad, and I wonder if he's on work experience. I look at my amazing daughter and – like I do every single day – count my blessings. We have almost lost her so many times. Yet here she is, my strong, beautiful fourteen-year-old, calmly explaining her illness. Tiny silver earrings shimmer from under her brown hair, which is loose around her shoulders.

'A normal heart pumps blood around your body,' she is saying. 'But my heart was too weak to do that properly, so my body wasn't getting the blood it needed. I've always known I would need a heart transplant one day.'

When the local paper called last week about doing a story on Meg's new heart, I wasn't sure. 'What if it makes her stressed?' I said to Steve.

'Then we stop the interview.' He looked at me, seeing the uncertainty in my face. 'It's up to Meg, Lizzie.'

'I want to do it,' she said, the second we asked her. 'I want to show other sick kids what's possible.'

Meg has always been positive, even when she was too ill to go to school, or to play with her friends. Even when she only had enough energy to lie in bed, too tired even to lift the TV remote.

'And how does it feel,' the reporter says now, 'to have someone else's heart?'

This is the bit of the story they really want. The rest – Meg's cancer, her heart problem – is just background. There are two hundred heart transplants each year in the UK, and only a handful of those are for children. Meg is a success story. Meg is a miracle. Our miracle.

The papers could fill their pages with Meg's life and they'd still only know the half of it – what it's been like, always knowing that Meg's heart might give up at any moment. She was on the waiting list for six months, all the time getting more and more sick. Then, on a day just like any other, we got the call, and everything changed.

'We've got a match.'

They had found one. The right size, the right blood group . . . the right heart for Meg. It was really happening. Meg's second chance at life. I felt excited and sick all at once, and I ran upstairs and pulled open Meg's door. She knew, the second she saw my face.

'They've got one, haven't they?'

Suddenly it hit home. Meg was going under the knife. Hours in an operating theatre, with all the risks that carried . . .

'It'll be okay, Mum,' Meg said, and I thought how wrong it was that she was the one reassuring me.

She was in theatre for four hours, but it felt like four days. Steve and I sat in the hospital canteen as other people came and went, staring at the bleeper they had given us to let us know when it was over.

'It must be strange,' the reporter says now.

For the first time in the interview, Meg stops to think. She puts a hand on her chest, to where the scars are hidden by her hoodie. I feel my own chest tighten. She's been through so much.

'It is a bit,' Meg admits. 'But without this heart I would have died. Feeling a bit strange is better than being a lot dead.' She grins, and I can tell that the reporter isn't sure whether to laugh. Meg's black humour takes a bit of getting used to.

'Um . . . wow, yeah, right,' he says. He frowns at his notebook, finding his next question. 'What would you like to say to people reading this story?' he asks. His pen hovers above the page.

'To join the organ register,' Meg says, right away.

I never even knew about the organ register, till Meg got sick. Now, we're all on it: Steve, me, all our friends, all Meg's friends. Your liver and kidneys are no good to you once you're dead, but they could keep someone else alive.

The reporter is almost done. 'Do you have a message for your donor's family?'

I keep thinking about the person who used to have Meg's heart. What would have happened if he hadn't joined the register?

'Just "thank you",' Meg says, and her eyes fill with tears. I put my arm round her and squeeze her tight. We don't know who Meg's heart came from. We know he was male, and that he died in an accident, and we know he was healthy. That's it. We don't know how old he was, or where he lived, or what sort of family he was from. It doesn't matter, I suppose. It only matters that, before he died, he ticked that box to say he was happy for someone to have his organs. And I thank my lucky stars every day that he did.

The article is in the local paper on Friday, with a big picture of Meg holding a red, heart-shaped helium balloon. *Thank you for my heart*, reads the headline. Meg beams from the photo – so different to the pale, thin girl of six months ago. I add my silent thanks to Meg's printed words.

I'm not working today. I used to be a teaching assistant in a primary school up the road, but I had to stop when Meg got sick. Since then I've picked up shifts where I can at the chocolate factory on the edge of town. We pack posh chocs into shiny gold boxes with black ribbons, and they don't mind how much we chat, as long as the job gets done. The chocolates have to be perfect to go in the boxes, and any that aren't go into the staff shop. A pound a bag – and you get a lot in a bag. Needless to say, Meg loves it.

I've promised to take her into town this afternoon to spend her birthday money, so I take a couple of hours in the morning to get the house straight. Steve is a roofer, and in the summer he works long hours, because in the winter he can't. We don't see him till eight or nine most evenings from June till September, and he's fit for nothing but tea in front of the telly. So I do the housework. He helps out a bit more in the winter, so it all evens out.

At eleven my friend Samira drops by on her way to work.

'Coffee?' I ask, as we walk through to the kitchen.

'You bet. It's been a hell of a week.'

Samira was Meg's nurse. We became friendly in the days after Meg's surgery, when Meg drifted in and out of sleep. Samira would join me for a cuppa when the ward was quiet. We stayed in touch after Meg came home, and I know Samira has a soft spot for the girl she calls her 'star patient'.

'Did you lose someone?' I say it quietly, even though Meg is upstairs.

Samira nods.

'I'm sorry.' I don't ask who died, or how. Samira wouldn't tell me, even if I did. I put a mug of coffee – white, one sugar – on the table, and push the tin of biscuits towards her. I couldn't do her job. For every life they save, there's another they don't.

Samira picks up the newspaper, folded so Meg's article is on top. 'How's she doing?'

'Some days you'd never even know she'd had surgery. She's going back to school next week.' For two whole years Meg hardly went to school, and in the six months since her transplant she hasn't been at all. A tutor worked with her in hospital and at home, but she's missed a lot. 'She has to do year nine again, but she's got a great bunch of friends – they won't leave her out.'

Samira is reading the article. 'This is lovely. You must be very proud of her.'

'I am.' I look upside down at the article I've already read a dozen times. *Fourteen-year-old Megan Thomas owes her life to a stranger*, it starts. 'I wish we knew more about him,' I say.

Samira holds up one hand, palm towards me. 'I can't tell you anything, you know that.'

'Even just a name would—'

'Lizzie, I can't.'

We're interrupted by the sound of feet on the stairs, and Meg comes into the kitchen. 'Mum, can I have—' she stops short, her face breaking into a grin when she sees who is here. 'Samira!'

Our friend stands, wrapping Meg up in her arms. 'You look *amazing*,' she tells her.

'That,' Meg says, 'is because I *am* amazing.' She pulls away and gives a twirl, then pats her chest. 'Still beating.'

'I should hope so too. Any pain?'

'None.'

'Out of breath?'

'Nope.'

'And you're doing your physiotherapy exercises?'

Meg rolls her eyes. 'You're as bad as Mum. Yes, I'm doing my physio.'

This eye-rolling is all for show, like a panto where she's playing the part of a teenager. Meg does her exercises every day. She takes her medication, eats properly, goes to bed when she's tired. She's the model patient.

'I have someone else's heart,' she said, when she came home from hospital. 'I have to look after it.'

'Good girl,' Samira says now. 'Oh – I almost forgot.' She slips an envelope out of her bag. 'Happy birthday – sorry it's late.'

Meg opens the card, her eyes lighting up as she spots the gift card for her favourite store. 'Thank you!'

'You shouldn't have,' I tell Samira, but she just winks at me, then drains her coffee.

'I'd better get to work.'

Meg and I have a lovely afternoon walking around the shops. She spends her birthday money. When she spots a top she loves but can't afford, I help out with a little extra we can't really spare. I'd love to be able to spoil her. I'd love to be able to take her on holiday. I look at photos on Facebook of sick kids who get taken to Disneyworld, or go swimming with dolphins, and I wonder what Meg really thinks of our long weekend in Bournemouth.

Steve is working the next day, but on Sunday I cook a roast and we settle down to watch a film together. Meg's phone lights up every few minutes, and she taps in a message, one eye still on the TV. Steve is nodding off, his head tipped back and his mouth open. Meg is just like him – the same straight nose, the same dimple in the left cheek. I stop watching the film and instead watch my daughter and my husband, my gaze falling first on one and then the other. I feel a warm glow inside. My family are the world to me.

I've got a late shift at the factory on Monday, starting two hours before Steve is due home. It's not ideal, leaving Meg alone, but I'm five minutes away, and she can text if she needs me. I'm running late. As I race out of the door, shouting a 'bye, love!' at Meg as I go, I see that Meg has picked up the post and left it on the table. I pick up a letter addressed to me and stuff it into my bag. I glance at it a couple of times as I drive to work. The envelope is cream, and the address handwritten, so it isn't a bill, or junk mail, or one of those charity appeals with a pen and a book of raffle tickets. A wedding invitation? Christening? I think hard, but can't think of anyone in our group of friends who might be sending us an invite.

It bugs me all the way to work so, when I get there, instead of clocking in and finding my white coat and daft hairnet, I stay in my car. I rip open the envelope and pull out the thick, expensive cream paper inside.

It's a letter. *Dear Lizzie*, it says. *I saw the article in the paper. I'm so happy to see your daughter doing so well.* I frown, confused, then read on. *I miss my son every day, and I'd do anything to have him back, but he would be so happy to know he saved a life.*

A prickle creeps across the back of my neck. *He saved a life.* I know exactly who this letter is from. I shouldn't read it. I should give it to Samira, and tell her to pass on a message. We've been told not to try to track down Meg's donor, that it will get complicated, but part of me so badly wants to know more about him . . .

Your daughter is beautiful, the letter says. *I only wish Jake could see her.*

Jake.

That's his name. The owner of Meg's heart. The man I owe everything to.

No, not man. *Boy.* Because this letter is from his mother. Karen Edwards. I feel a lurch in my chest as I think about what it took for her to write this

10

letter. She had to find me from the details in the newspaper, and sit at a desk, writing. Finding the words.

I sit in my car, the letter in my hands, staring at the final line of the letter.

Please, Lizzie, could I possibly meet Meg?

Chapter 2

Saying Thank You

'You can't write back.' Steve puts a mouthful of pork chop and mash in his mouth and chews. He waves his fork around, stressing his point.

'It feels rude not to.' We're eating late, and without Meg, who had beans on toast at seven, then went to her bedroom to watch something on her laptop.

'Maybe we should talk to Samira about it.'

I almost choke on my chop. 'No way.'

'Why not?'

'Because I know what she'll say.'

'Well then . . .'

We eat in silence for a bit, but I can't get the words in the letter out of my head. *I miss my son every day.* Somewhere, out there, is a mother going through everything I have dreaded for the last fourteen years. A mother who has taken her child to hospital, sat with them as they faded, and begged God or fate to keep them alive.

Please, Lizzie, could I possibly meet Meg?

Meg lived, because of this boy. Because of this mother, too, who supported her son's choice to donate his organs. How can I throw that lifeline back in her face?

The next day I pop into the hospital. I take some board games I cleared out from home, to give me an excuse to go into the family room. Samira ducks out of the ward for a moment, rolling her shoulders and stretching her back, which is stiff from bending over patients.

'Oh, hey,' I say, as if I only just thought of it, 'do families ever send cards? You know, to be passed on?'

Samira narrows her eyes slightly. 'Sometimes.'

'And do you pass them on?'

'Of course, but we take out names, addresses, anything personal first. Why do you ask?'

'Oh, Meg wanted to know.' I feel myself blush at the lie.

Samira narrows her eyes. 'Lizzie, trust me: getting to know the relatives of someone who gave you an organ is a really bad idea. It creates all sorts of feelings of guilt. People think they need to repay such a huge act of kindness. But the whole point of giving an organ is that it's done without any desire for reward. It's the most selfless thing you can ever do.' Her face softens and she touches my arm lightly. 'Look, I'll pass on anything you want to give me – but leave out your name and address, okay?'

I blush again, letting her think that she's right. One thing is certain – I can't tell Samira that Karen Edwards has sent us a letter.

I bring up the subject with Meg on Wednesday, when Steve is at work, and we're out the back of the house. The garden of our two-bed terraced house is tiny, with a square of lawn Steve mows on Sundays, and a little patio with a table and chairs. Around the lawn are borders, only a foot deep, but filled with colour. I kneel on the ground and pick at the tiny weeds around the geraniums.

Meg is lying on the grass, her T-shirt rolled up to expose a flat, tanned stomach. She's touchy about her scar, which runs in a deep groove from her neck to just above her belly button, but at home she doesn't care. I hope that, in time, she'll relax in public, too, and see her scar for what it is – a sign of survival.

'I got a letter on Monday,' I start. 'From the mum of the boy who gave you your heart.'

Meg sits up, her mouth open. 'Can we meet her?'

'That's what she'd like.' I hesitate. 'You know we're not supposed to? Samira says—'

'It isn't Samira's heart,' Meg says strongly. 'It's mine.' Her eyes flash. I should be leading her up the right path, I know, not pressing her to go against Samira's advice. But . . . Meg knows her own mind. She's a young woman who wouldn't be here without the kindness of a stranger. And now she wants to say thank you.

'Okay,' I say. 'Let's do it.'

Karen didn't put a phone number in her letter, so I write back to the address at the top of the page. She lives in a town about an hour from us. I suggest meeting halfway in a café on a retail park. I give her my mobile number, and two days later I get a text.

Thank you so much – you don't know what this means to me. See you on Saturday. Karen xx

I feel warm inside. We owe everything to this woman, and it feels good to do something – however small – to say thank you.

Steve isn't coming.

'I'm working,' he said, but it isn't only that. He thinks I'm making a mistake.

'Karen just wants to see the life her son saved,' I said. 'It's a sort of closure for her.' And for me, I think. In many ways Meg has coped better than

15

me with the transplant. Like her dad, she's focused on the future, but I can't stop dwelling on the past. I'm hoping that meeting Karen will change that, and I can start to move on.

We get to the café early, and I switch off the engine and look at Meg. 'Ready?'

She nods, her eyes shining with a mixture of excitement and nerves. 'Ready.'

I see Karen straight away. She isn't the only woman sitting on her own, but she's the only woman with eyes so full of pain it hurts to look at them. The only woman whose grief can be seen in the hollows of her cheeks and the shadows beneath her eyes.

She stands up as we walk towards her table, and her bottom lip trembles. She opens her mouth, but nothing comes out, and I'm struggling too, because what is there to say? What could ever be enough?

It's Meg who finds a way. Meg who steps forward, who gently takes Karen's hand and places it flat against her own chest and holds it firmly in place. Meg is trembling, and I move to stand next to her, one hand on the small of her back. Karen's face pales. She closes her eyes and I think that perhaps she is going to faint, but a sad smile tugs at the corners of her mouth.

'Jake,' she whispers.

'Thank you for my heart,' Meg says softly. And we stand there, the three of us, forever linked by the heart beating beneath Karen's fingers.

The sound of someone clearing their throat jolts us into action. I turn to see a waitress staring at us in alarm. She must wonder what on earth we're doing.

'Can I get you anything?'

'Tea, please.' Karen and I speak at the same time, and we laugh, the awkward tension disappearing. We sit at the table where Karen's jacket is slung over a chair.

'How about you, love?' I ask Meg. 'Diet Coke?'

She takes a moment to answer. 'I think I'd like a coffee, actually.'

I widen my eyes. 'You don't drink coffee.'

'I know, but I've been craving it for ages – it's really weird.'

'I used to say Jake was powered by coffee, he drank so much.' Karen smiles bravely.

Meg turns to her. 'Tell me about him. What was he like?'

'He was seventeen – he'd just passed his test – and he loved messing about with cars. He was always out in the garage, hands covered in grease.' *Ga-rarge*, she said, with an 'ah' in the middle. She has a beautiful voice, clear and rich, with every letter given a place. Posh, I suppose you'd call her. Her handbag has the glossy sheen of an expensive brand, and the lining of her jacket is so lovely you could wear it inside out. I bite my lip, feeling awkward in my Primark cardigan.

Karen is telling Meg about Jake's love of practical jokes, about his DVD collection, and how gentle he always was with her sister's children. Shyly, she taps her phone and tilts the screen to show Meg. 'Here he is.' Her voice cracks on the final word.

I lean across and see a handsome boy grinning at the camera. He's in one of those long thin boats you see on the river, pushing a pole into the water.

'He—' Karen struggles to get out the words. 'He had a place . . . at Oxford university.'

My eyes fill with tears, and suddenly it doesn't matter that Karen speaks posher than I do. It doesn't matter that her handbag cost more than all my clothes. I still have my child, and she lost hers. I push back my chair with a scrape, and bend awkwardly by her chair, wrapping her up in a hug. 'I'm so sorry you lost him.'

There's another cough. The waitress is standing with our drinks, looking even more confused than when she took our order.

'Sorry,' I say, with an awkward laugh. 'It's all a bit emotional here.'

We stay in the café for two hours, talking and crying, and ordering more pots of tea. My stomach rumbles and I realise it's lunchtime. I glance at the list of sandwiches, chalked onto a blackboard above the counter. Karen follows my gaze.

'Shall we have something to eat?' she says. 'My treat.'

'Oh no, I'll get this,' I say quickly, even though we can't afford to eat out whenever we want to.

'I insist.' Karen moves a hand across the table to touch mine. 'You don't know what it means to me, to meet Meg, to feel Jake's heart keeping her alive.' She stops short, her lips pulled thin as if she's holding back tears.

'Well then,' I say. 'That would be lovely. Thank you.'

Karen has a roast beef sandwich, and I order soup. Meg asks for baked beans on toast, and I give a short laugh. 'Surprise surprise.' I catch Karen's eye and explain. 'It's all she's wanted since the transplant. She barely touched them before.'

Karen takes a sharp intake of breath. Her face has turned pale.

'What is it? What's wrong?'

'Nothing, it's just . . .' Karen shivers, like someone just walked over her grave. 'First the coffee, now baked beans . . .'

'Did Jake like beans?'

'He loved them,' Karen said. 'One Christmas we went to one of those cash–and-carry places and wrapped up a huge tin of them – the sort they buy in restaurants. A stupid joke, but . . .' She's on the edge of tears again, but this time I don't move to comfort her. A prickle of unease moves across the back of my neck.

Steve and I joked about Meg's sudden craving for beans. We knew from Samira that transplant patients often behave differently after surgery.

'It's a very traumatic process,' she told us. 'A big change for both mind and body, so you should be prepared to see some changes in Meg.'

It never occurred to me that the cravings – the differences – might not have come from the surgery, but from the heart itself.

'It's called cell memory,' Karen says, as if she can read my mind. Her gaze is intense, and I have to force myself to hold it. 'The organ holds on to the features of the person it came from, and transfers them to the new body. There are lots of studies on it.'

The new body. My blood runs cold. *Meg*, I want to say, *her name is Meg*. But I don't. I listen to Karen tell me incredible stories of transplant patients who find they can speak languages they've never learned, and remember places they've never visited. Surely that isn't possible?

'Doctors can't explain it,' Karen says, 'but too many people have seen it, for it not to be real. Some things are bigger than science.'

Meg is wide-eyed. I squeeze her hand. 'Don't let it worry you, love.'

'Worry me?' She frowns, confused at my words. 'It's *incredible!*' She looks at Karen, and one hand creeps to her chest. 'It's like I'm two people now. Me, and Jake.' Tears spring to her eyes, and when I look at Karen I see she's crying too.

And suddenly I have the strangest feeling that they are the mother and daughter, and I am the outsider. I force a smile, and eat my lunch. Karen finds tissues and hands one to Meg, who blows her nose, then tucks in to her beans.

'Could we . . .' Karen says hesitantly, when we've finished eating. 'Could we do this again sometime?'

No.

The voice whispers in my head, taking me by surprise. Where did that come from? Karen's son saved Meg's life – why shouldn't she see Meg again?

Say no.

The voice is urgent, like the feeling in your chest when you walk past a dark alley late at night, or step too close to the cliff edge on a summer walk. But those reasons are valid. Sensible. You can see the risks. Why am I hearing a warning now?

'I know we're not supposed to,' Karen says, a flush filling her cheeks, 'but I'm finding things so hard without Jake and Michael—' She breaks off, pressing her lips together as if she's holding back a sob.

'Michael?' I glance at Meg, who gives a tiny shake of her head. She doesn't know either. This is the first time Karen has mentioned a Michael.

Karen takes a deep breath, then looks up. 'My husband,' she says softly. 'He was in the accident with Jake. I lost both my boys that day.'

I bring my hands to my mouth, but I can't stop the cry that escapes me. Life is so unfair. That poor woman. I try to imagine life without Steve and Meg, but I can't – my world would be empty without them.

'Of course you can see Meg again,' I say.

I ignore the voice in my head that tells me I've made a terrible, terrible mistake.

Chapter 3

Helping Out

I blink my eyes, gritty from staring at a screen for too long. I've been reading about cell memory, and my head is spinning. The article I've just read is about a woman in America who got a heart from a man who was shot in the face. Soon after the operation – without knowing anything about the man who died – she began having nightmares about flashes of light, fired at her face.

Another article told of a vegetarian who suddenly craved meat, and a footballer who got keen on dancing. Features that had clung to the hearts as they were removed, only to be passed to their new owners.

'It's not possible,' I say out loud. I'm no scientist, but surely cravings for salt and vinegar crisps aren't held in an organ's DNA?

But there's no doubt about it. Meg has changed. She's a night-owl, when she used to be a lark. She's drinking coffee, when she used to drink tea, and

Irn-Bru, instead of Diet Coke. All her life she's wanted to be a teacher, now suddenly she's looking at courses to teach outdoor pursuits.

'It's all perfectly normal,' Samira says, when I share my concerns. 'A big operation makes patients look at their lives – they often change direction.'

Jake liked outdoor pursuits, I want to say. But I can't tell her I ignored everything she told me, and answered Karen's letter. I can't tell her we met up, that Karen bought us lunch, that I've agreed to see her again. I can't tell her any of that.

'There's absolutely no evidence that cell memory is real,' Samira says.

'Then how do you explain the case studies I read?' I tell her about the gunshot to the face, and the dancing footballer.

Samira sighs. 'Nurses talk. Doctors, too. They're not supposed to, but it happens. Snippets of detail here and there, in the operating theatre, on the wards. Patients don't even know they're hearing it, but they pick up bits. Later, their mind spits it back out again like it's coming straight from them.'

I want to believe her. I don't want to think that, inside Meg, beats a heart that carries enough of Jake's personality to change my little girl's.

'Your footballer,' Samira says, 'he probably heard someone talking about a dancer as he was going under.'

'Okay,' I say slowly, 'but why would the doctors talk about someone liking beans. Why would they even know that about a donor?'

Samira laughs. 'Lots of kids like beans, Lizzie.'

'Meg used to hate them.'

'So she's changed her mind! There's nothing to suggest that came from Meg's donor.'

I let it drop. I can't push any further in case Samira begins to wonder.

The following Sunday I'm cooking tea – if you can call bunging a frozen pizza in the oven cooking – when the doorbell rings.

'Can you get that, love?' I ask Steve.

He's home early for a change, and I promised Meg she could choose tea. I'm normally quite strict about meat and two veg, but pizza and chips doesn't hurt once in a while. Call it a celebration for Meg's first week back at school.

I check the chips and turn them over so they crisp up nicely. I hear the front door open, then voices, too quiet for me to hear above the extractor fan. It'll be the Red Cross people – they dropped in an envelope earlier this week. I look around the kitchen but can't see it. Bugger. Now we'll have to give them a quid, instead of shoving in a few coppers and handing it back sealed.

I bend down to put the chips back in the oven,

just as Steve comes into the kitchen. 'There's a pound coin in my purse,' I say, without looking.

'Hello, Lizzie.'

I'm so surprised I let go of the baking tray, burning the back of my hand on the rack above it. 'Shit!' I snatch it back, cradling it in my other hand as I stand up, closing the oven door with my foot.

Karen Edwards is standing in the door of my kitchen, her face a study of concern. 'You need to get that under the cold tap,' she says. When I don't move, she crosses the kitchen and steers me firmly to the sink, running the tap and holding my wrist so the water cascades over the burn.

'I – I'm fine,' I say, when I'm able to speak. My hand throbs, but it isn't the burn that's closing my throat, making it hard to form words. It's Karen's grip, tight around my wrist, holding me in place. She's so close I can smell her perfume – musky, expensive – and feel the swing of her hair on my neck.

'Do you have a first aid kit?' She's talking to Steve, as if I'm a child.

'Um, I don't think so.'

Karen makes a faint tutting noise – so faint that I'm not sure if I've imagined it.

'It's in the bathroom,' I say, although the shelf of out-of-date aspirin and dusty dressings can hardly be called a 'kit'. 'But really, I'm fine.' I turn off the tap with my free hand and turn my body so Karen has to release me. 'This is a surprise.' I paste a smile on my face.

'You don't mind, do you? My dropping in, like this?' She addresses her question to Steve, whose reply is polite, even though I can see the doubt in his eyes. I didn't tell him Karen wanted to see Meg again, and I don't know what he'll say if Karen brings it up now.

'Of course not. It's good to meet you.' There's an awkward pause. 'Um, I'll tell Meg you're here.'

No!

It's still there – the warning voice in my head that I can't explain. I remind myself of everything Karen has lost, and paste a smile on my face. 'Cup of tea?'

'Lovely.'

Karen looks around the kitchen as I boil the kettle, her gaze resting on the calendar, the photographs on the fridge, the pile of bills on the side.

'Pizza for supper?' she says, seeing the boxes.

'We hardly ever have it,' I say quickly.

'Everything in small amounts, isn't that what they say?' She's agreeing with me, so why does it feel like a criticism?

There is a sound of running feet on the stairs, and Meg bursts into the kitchen. 'Karen!' They

27

hug, then Karen puts a hand flat on Meg's collarbone. They exchange a smile, then Karen takes back her hand. The whole thing lasts only a few seconds, but I can tell that this is a ritual, now. Karen will feel Jake's heart every time she sees Meg. It's why she came.

'Are you staying for tea?' Meg says.

Karen looks at me. 'Oh, I don't think—'

'There's plenty, isn't there, Mum?'

I'm cornered. 'Masses. Do stay, Karen.'

So she stays. Not that she eats much. She pushes her chips around her plate, and cuts up her pizza into tiny pieces, leaving the stuffed crust for Steve to eye hungrily.

'I've been googling what you said about cell memory,' Meg says. I look up in surprise. I haven't said anything to Meg about my own research, and only mentioned it to Steve in passing. 'It's incredible,' she adds. Looking at me and her dad in turn, she begins to tell us about the exact same case studies I spoke to Samira about. 'And she *actually* saw the gunshots in her dream,' Meg finishes, with a dramatic flourish.

'How weird,' Steve says. I had expected him to shoot the theory down in flames, but there's no hint of disbelief in his face, only amazement. Despite him telling me it was a bad idea for me and Meg to meet Karen, there's no sign of concern now. He's not one for small talk, but now he's chatting away to Karen like they're best mates. I feel a prickle of jealousy.

'Have you noticed any other changes since your transplant, Meg?' Karen has put her knife and fork together, her plate still almost as full as when I set it down. 'You mentioned the cravings for beans, and the changes to your body clock – is there anything else? Are you watching the same sorts of things on television, for example?'

Meg thinks, a piece of salami speared on her waiting fork. 'I ended up watching a Western the other night, when I couldn't sleep, and I was surprised by how into it I was!' She laughs, but Karen lets out a little sound, halfway between a breath and a cry.

'Jake loved Westerns. Always did. Anything with Clint Eastwood, in particular.'

Meg stares at her, open-mouthed. 'This had Clint Eastwood in it!'

So do eighty per cent of the Westerns they show on Freeview, I think.

Karen holds up both hands in an *I rest my case* sort of way, and I glance at Steve. He's looking at Meg with a new expression in his eyes, like he's never seen her before. I know that face. It mirrors my own. Meg is our daughter. We've known her for fourteen years – we know her better than anyone else. But now it's like she's becoming someone else.

It's ridiculous.

Isn't it?

'PJs and teeth,' I tell Meg, catching sight of the clock. 'School tomorrow.'

'Inset day,' she says, gleefully.

'Since when?'

She looks sheepish. 'Um, since the letter they sent home that might still be in my bag . . .'

'Meg!' I look at Steve. 'I've got a double shift tomorrow. We need—' I bite off the end of my sentence, not wanting to let Karen know that money is tight. 'I can't let them down,' I finish, instead.

'I can't take a day off, love, not halfway through a build.'

'Meg can come to me,' Karen says. 'It would be no trouble – I'm not doing anything I can't re-arrange.'

'I really don't think . . .' I look at Steve, expecting him to back me up, but he's looking at Karen as if she's offered him a million pounds.

'That's really generous of you, Karen,' he says.

'We can go shopping! What do you think, Meg?'

It's obvious from Meg's face what her answer is going to be, even before she shouts 'Yes please!' And then she starts planning the shops they could visit and the clothes they could try on.

'That's settled, then,' Karen says, with a smile, and we thank her.

Later, when she gets in her car to go home, we stand in the hall with the door open.

'You've changed your tune,' I say to Steve, while Meg's out front, saying goodbye again.

He shrugs. 'I don't know what I was worried about. She's really nice.'

But I can't shake the unease I feel. Karen gave Meg her son's heart. She bought us lunch. Now she's helping us out with childcare.

What will she want in return?

Chapter 4

Coming Between Us

Meg has a great day with Karen. When I get home from the factory, my feet aching, she's still buzzing. I've brought her back some chocolates – paid extra for the posh ones with cream filling and shards of ginger on top. But, when I see the heap of plastic bags on Meg's bed, I drop the battered box back into my bag.

'Karen bought you clothes?'

'I didn't ask, I promise.' Meg pulls on a black denim jacket and gives me a twirl. 'She insisted.' The jacket looks expensive, with artful rips at the elbows and careful fraying around the collar. 'And there's *this* to go with it, and *this* . . .' She holds up a series of garments – a patterned dress, a pair of boots, a soft grey vest top with THIS GIRL CAN across the front in neon letters.

'It's too much,' I tell Steve, when I'm back downstairs. I don't trust myself to say what I want to say if I call Karen, so I text her instead. I compose the message carefully, reading and re-reading to make sure the balance is right. Grateful, but firm.

Thank you so much for today – it really helped us out. Meg had a lovely day. Please let me know what the clothes came to and I'll give you the money x

The answer comes swiftly. *My treat! X*

I can't let you do that, I text back.

This time there's a longer pause. *I don't have a child to spoil any more,* she says eventually. *Please let me spoil yours instead xx*

How can I say no to that?

Meg wears her new clothes until they practically walk into the washing machine on their own. She stops watching *X Factor* with me and Steve, and instead downloads old black-and-white Westerns onto her laptop and watches them in her room.

'I'm worried about her,' I tell Steve. 'She seems so . . . different.'

'She's happy, though,' he says. And I can't argue with that.

Over the next few weeks I manage to put Karen out of my mind. The leaves are starting to fall and, with them, my thoughts turn to Christmas. It's still weeks away, but presents won't buy themselves, and if we want a decent tree and a turkey I'll need to put in some more hours at work. The shorter days mean Steve stops work at four, every job taking twice as many days as it would have in the summer, so I take evening shifts to make ends meet. It's not ideal – I race out of the door just as Steve comes in – but at least Meg gets one of us at home all the time.

On Thursday, I come home at ten-thirty p.m. to find a car in my spot outside the house. A sleek black Audi, with leather seats and a stitched steering wheel. I recognise it instantly, and my stomach twists into knots.

Karen is on the sofa, a mug of tea in her hand, and her feet curled up beneath her. She's wearing a black wrap dress, and has her hair tied in a loose knot on one side of her neck. Steve is in his armchair, turned to face her, and although the TV is on, the sound is off. I stand in the hall, watching them for a moment, feeling like a spy.

'Here she is!' Karen says, making me wonder if they've been talking about me. 'How was the chocolate factory?' She makes it sound like a joke – like it's a place I've made up.

'It was . . . fine. I . . . I wasn't expecting company tonight.' It's Steve I'm really talking to, but when I look at him he won't meet my eyes.

'Karen brought something round for Meg,' he says.

More presents? 'That's really kind of you, but—'

'She won't thank me for this one!' Karen laughs.

She picks up a Boots carrier bag from the cushion next to her and holds it open so I can see the contents. 'Multivitamins, extra iron, vitamin K and arnica. Good for blood flow. Poor Meg will rattle when she walks.' She laughs again, and this time Steve joins in.

'She's taking a lot of pills already,' I say. The bottles are in the bathroom, their labels filled with long names I can't pronounce.

'These are supplements. They'll help Meg stay healthy.'

'She *is* healthy. She's doing really well. The consultant said so.' I don't mean to sound so abrupt, but Steve turns to look at me, a shocked expression on his face.

'Lizzie!'

'I got another present too.' Karen is less sure of herself now. She moves her legs from beneath her and sits upright. She takes a postcard-sized envelope from the carrier bag and hands it to me. I open it. Inside is a picture of vegetables – carrots, potatoes, beans.

'I don't understand.'

'It's an organic vegetable box. It'll come once a week – it's all paid for.'

Rage builds inside me, and I fight to contain it. 'You don't think I feed my family properly?'

'Of course! I just—'

'We don't need charity!'

'It's not—'

'Lizzie! Karen has done a lovely thing – the least you can do is say thank you.' I've never seen Steve like this, flushed and angry, his jaw tight with tension. Karen stands, slipping on her shoes and picking up her bag. She leaves the Boots bag on the sofa.

'I was just doing what we mums do best,' she says quietly, looking at me squarely. I'm shocked to see tears welling up in her eyes. 'Taking good care of our kids.'

Steve follows her to the front door, and I hear him saying sorry, and her telling him *it's fine, don't worry, she's been through a lot.*

Guilt seeps into me like water into a sponge. I might have been through a lot, but Karen has been through worse. I pick up Steve's glass of wine and drain it. When I turn round, he's standing in the doorway, watching me.

'She's a nice woman,' he says. 'She did a nice thing – and God knows, we could do with the help right now.'

'We're doing all right.'

'We're barely scraping by!' He follows me to the kitchen.

'You didn't even want me to meet her,' I say, refilling the empty glass.

'I was worried, that's all. About going against Samira's advice. But Karen is nice – I like her.'

'Clearly! I come home from work, and the two of you are cosying up on the sofa!' My voice rises until I'm almost shouting, and I wait for Steve to shout back. But he doesn't. Instead he looks at me sadly.

'Can you even imagine what that woman has been through?' he says. 'What it must be like to see Meg, smiling, laughing, going shopping? Can you imagine the strength Karen has to be a friend to us, when all the time she must be thinking "Jake should be here"?'

I open my mouth to defend myself, but can't find the words.

Steve turns and leaves the room, and I hear his soft tread on the stairs. And for the first time in the twenty years we've been married, he sleeps in the spare room.

Chapter 5

From Bad to Worse

When I get up the next day, Steve has already left for work. Meg surfaces at eight, and I chivvy her through breakfast and into her school uniform.

'Did you and Dad have a row last night?'

'Why do you say that?'

'I heard shouting.'

'You should have been asleep.'

'So you did have a row.'

'Eat your cereal,' I say, putting a bowl in front of her. On the counter, next to the kettle, Steve has laid out the vitamins Karen brought round. I think about sweeping the whole lot into the bin. But she didn't bring them for me, did she? She brought them for Meg. To keep her healthy. What kind of mum would get in the way of that?

'Earth to Lizzie . . .' Samira taps my arm.

'Sorry – what were you saying?' We're grabbing a coffee between my factory shift and Samira's hospital one, and I know I haven't been my usual self. I keep running over everything I said to Karen last night – everything Steve said to me. Did I over-react? Was Steve right to be angry with me? I've tried calling him twice, but he hasn't picked up. That's not unusual – it's hard to take calls when you're on a roof with a stack of tiles – but today it feels personal.

'It doesn't matter. Are you all right?'

I pause, working out what I can safely say. 'Steve slept in the spare room last night.'

Samira raises an eyebrow.

'It'll blow over,' I say.

'It's not like you two to argue.'

It isn't. Life's too short. We, of all people, know that. I can count the rows Steve and I have had on two hands, but it isn't the harsh words that have upset me the most. It's the sadness I saw in Steve's eyes when I threw Karen's gift back in her face. He thought I was a horrible person.

Am I?

'How's work?' I ask Samira, keen to change the subject.

'Same old. I've been roped in to running a fund-raising evening – because I've got loads of spare time on my hands, right?' She grins.

'I'll help,' I say quickly. 'I could make cakes? Maybe ask my boss for a raffle prize?' I'm making amends for last night's behaviour, although Samira isn't to know that.

'You're a star. Thank you.'

When I get home there's a parcel in the porch. I frown as I pick it up, wondering what it is. As I carry it inside, I realise. It's Karen's organic veg box.

I have to admit, it's impressive. The thick cardboard box is stuffed full of fresh fruit – crisp apples and ripe bananas, and something I think is a mango. The vegetables are huge, and just as fresh. There's a bunch of carrots, with trailing green tops, and a huge onion, sitting on top of a bag of spinach. There's garlic and beetroot, and a load of salad – it'll do us for a week, easy.

I roll up my sleeves and set to work. By the time Meg's home from school – Steve following not long after – the kitchen is filled with the smell of vegetable curry simmering. A pan of rice waits in cold water on the hob.

'Something smells good.' Steve's tone is wary. He doesn't kiss me, the way he usually does, and I see Meg glance anxiously between us.

'How was your day?' I ask her.

'Good. I'm going to try out for hockey. Karen says I can have Jake's stick.'

'Hockey?' I wipe my hands on a tea towel. 'I think it's a bit soon to be doing sport, love.'

'It's been almost eight months!'

'Wait till we see the consultant again, then we can talk to him about—'

'Dad!' Meg turns to Steve, who looks at me.

'She's doing well. Even Samira says so. You can't wrap her up in cotton wool for ever, Lizzie.'

'Cotton . . .' The words die on my lips as hot tears well in my eyes. I can't win. If I reject Karen's gifts because I feel she is butting into our lives, I don't care enough about my daughter. If I care too much, I'm wrapping her up in cotton wool. I throw the tea towel on the table. 'I'm going for a walk.'

I walk from the narrow streets of the estate where we live, to the wide, tree-lined avenues further out of town. Houses worth half a million – more. I bet Karen lives in a house like this, I think. I bet she's home now, wondering if her veg box arrived, and mentally ticking off her good deed for the day.

She lost her son and her husband.

The thought of that startles me, and I stop walking. What am I doing? Filled with resentment towards a woman who must be eaten up with grief. A woman who must cry herself to sleep at night?

I need to get over this.

I walk back faster, shivering as dusk falls, and I realise I walked out of the house without a coat.

When I get home, Steve says nothing. He dishes

up the supper I made, and the rice he cooked, and we eat in silence at the kitchen table.

'Well, this is fun,' Meg says, her voice thick with sarcasm. She excuses herself as soon as possible, scraping her plate – with most of the vegetables, I notice – into the food bin, before going to her room.

'I'm sorry,' I say, just as Steve's phone pings with a text message. I glance at the phone as he picks it up, but he angles the screen away. 'Who is it?'

'No one.' He taps out a response.

No one? I almost laugh. I expect that from Meg, but from Steve? I reach for the phone. He resists for a second, as my fingers wrap around it, then he shrugs and lets go.

He is texting Karen.

How is everything? she's written.

Not brilliant, is Steve's reply.

'You're telling her our business?' I can hardly get the words out.

Steve rubs his face and sighs, as if this is all very boring. 'She asked how things were, I told her. That's hardly "our business".' He makes air quotes with his fingers.

I push back my chair and it scrapes against the tiled floor. 'I hope you were comfortable in the spare room last night, because guess where you're sleeping tonight?'

*

42

I'm glad when the pale morning sun filters through the curtains in my bedroom, and I can finally give up on the pretence of sleep. I pad across the landing to Meg's room, and shake her gently.

'Time to get up, love.'

I pause by the closed door to the spare bedroom, wondering if Steve lay awake all night, if he's awake now. But when I get downstairs, he's in the kitchen, an empty cereal bowl in the sink, and a coffee mug rinsed out on the drainer. He's been up for a while.

'I'll take that apology any time you're ready,' he says.

My jaw drops. 'You what? You've got that the wrong way round. You're the one messaging Karen behind my back.'

'Behind your back?' Steve gives a bark of laughter. 'I text lots of people, Lizzie. Graham from footy. Sharon on payroll. My brother. Do you want me to run all those by you first, too?'

'You tried to hide it from me.'

'And you wonder why?' Steve waves an arm at me. 'I don't know what's got into you lately, Lizzie. You've got a bee in your bonnet about Karen, and it's turned you loopy.'

'If anyone is loopy,' I say, 'it's Karen. She's obsessed with Meg – can't you see?'

'She's missing her son.'

'That doesn't give her the right to mess with our lives!' I shout at him, blood rushing to my head. 'I wish we'd never met her, I wish she and her perfect bloody son were never even born—'

'Then Meg wouldn't have got a heart,' Steve starts, but I'm out of control, and I scream into his face.

'Better no heart than a heart from a family of crazies!'

I hear a noise behind me, like a stifled cry, and turn around to find Meg standing in the doorway to the kitchen, her eyes full of tears.

What am I doing?

My rage for Karen has made me say things I don't even mean.

'Meg—' I take a step towards her but she backs away, stumbling then turning around and running from the house, slamming the front door behind her.

'Let her go,' Steve says. 'School is probably the best place for her.'

'I can't bear to think of her upset all day.'

Steve opens his mouth, as if he's about to say *Well, whose fault is that?* Then he closes it again, perhaps thinking better of it. 'Call the head. Make sure she's okay. But leave her be for a bit, yeah?'

I nod, feeling numb with guilt.

Meg's teacher confirms she arrived safely in

school. She promises to call me if there are any problems, or if Meg seems upset. I don't have work today, so I clean the house from top to bottom, and make Meg's favourite pasta dish for tea. I even text Karen to tell her the veg box arrived – *so yummy, thank you! x*

At four p.m., twenty minutes after Meg normally gets home from school, I call her mobile. It's switched off – or out of battery, which isn't unusual. By four-fifteen, I'm pacing the kitchen, and by the time Steve gets in, at half four, I'm frantic with fear.

'Have you been out looking for her?' he says.

'I wanted to be here if she got back. Oh Steve, where is she? It'll be dark before too long.'

'Try her friends. Call me the second you hear anything.' He picks up his keys again and heads out. I scroll through my phone, calling the mums of friends Meg has had since primary school. I curse the nature of secondary school because I don't know half of the kids she hangs around with now. I text Karen, in case Meg has been in touch, but she doesn't reply.

Steve comes back an hour later, and I know from his face that he hasn't found her. 'I spoke to some kids hanging out at the park,' he said. 'I showed them a photo and gave them my number.' His face creases with worry. 'What if something has happened to her, Lizzie?'

I start to cry. 'I'm so sorry – this is all my fault.'

Steve steps forward, taking me in his arms and pressing my face against his broad chest. I hear the *thud thud* of his heart and think of the pills Meg needs to take every day to protect her from infection. I pull away. 'I'm calling the police.'

The officers come quickly, two women in black uniforms and stab vests. PCs Clarke and Stanford. They take the pictures we give them of Meg, and list the drugs she needs to take each morning. They write down the name of her school, of her friends, her consultant. They search her room and take the diary she hasn't written in since before her transplant.

'Does she have any mental health problems?' says PC Clarke.

'Any suicidal tendencies?' PC Stanford asks.

I sob as I tell them *no*, but admit that Steve and I had been rowing, that Meg had heard me say some things I didn't mean.

'I see,' PC Clarke said, writing something in her notebook, and I knew she thought it was my fault, too.

They leave us an hour later, promising updates when they have them, and telling us that officers are out looking for our little girl. They use terms like 'vulnerable' and 'high-risk', and each one feeds the fear inside me.

Suicidal tendencies.

What if Meg has hurt herself? What if someone has hurt her?

Steve and I cling to each other, our argument forgotten. It was stupid. Petty. When Meg comes back I'll apologise to her, explain that I lost the plot for a bit, but that everything's okay now. Mum and Dad love each other, and love her, and that's all that matters.

The phone rings at eleven. Steve picks it up and I hold my breath until he nods and says *yes, okay.* He puts down the phone.

'They've found her.'

Chapter 6

How the Other Half Live

You could fit the entire ground floor of our house into Karen's kitchen. I was wrong – she doesn't live on a tree-lined avenue. She lives at the end of her own bloody tree-lined drive, in a massive grey stone house with two bay trees in giant pots either side of the front door. Steve pulled up next to Karen's sleek Audi. The engine was still running as I flung off my seatbelt and ran to the front door.

'Meg!' I raised a hand to thump my fist on the glossy black paint, but the door opened before I had a chance, and I stumbled forward.

'Mrs Thomas?' It was PC Clarke. The same police officer who asked about Meg's mental health. The one who looked at me when I told her what Meg had overheard, and judged me for it.

'Where is she?' I said.

'Why don't you come through to the kitchen?'

Steve had caught up with me by then, and we followed PC Clarke to the kitchen, which is where we're all sitting now, like we're here for some sort of party.

'Where is she?'

'She's fine,' Karen says.

That isn't what I asked. Above the table is a huge canvas with a photo of Karen with Jake and a man who must be Michael. I look away. I don't want to feel sorry for Karen right now.

'Would you like some tea? The kettle's on.'

'No, I don't want bloody tea! I want to see my daughter.' The police officers have had tea, I notice. And I see the crumbs on the table by their mugs, that tell me they had biscuits, too. Biscuits!

PC Clarke takes charge.

'Meg is watching TV upstairs,' she says. 'I thought it would be a good idea to have a chat first, before we bring her down.'

'A chat? About what?' Steve is as confused as I am. Relief making us both terse and angry. He turns to Karen, and I think he's going to lay into her, but his tone softens a little as he speaks to her. 'You should have rung us, Karen – we were out of our mind with worry.'

Karen twists her hands in front of her, reddening slightly. 'I'm sorry. I wanted to – I really did, especially when I got your text, but Meg begged me not to, and . . .' She looks at the police officers.

'You did the right thing,' PC Stanford says.

She *what*? Anger rises inside me and I start to stand, pushing my chair back so it scrapes against Karen's expensive tiled floor. I catch an exchange of glances between the two police officers. Steve places a warning hand on my arm. Slowly, I lower myself back down. 'How,' I say, with as much control as I can manage, 'is not telling us where our missing child is, the "right thing"?'

'The welfare of the child is of the utmost importance,' says PC Stanford. 'Sometimes – and I'm not saying this is the case here – kids run away from home because of something that's happening there. Something the parents are doing.'

This time I push my chair back so violently it falls over, with a crash that echoes around Karen's starkly modern kitchen. 'Did you just accuse us of . . .' I can barely get the words out. 'Of *child abuse*?'

PC Stanford doesn't react. 'No,' she says calmly. 'I said *sometimes* kids are unhappy at home. And so the sensible thing is to let the authorities handle it.'

I stand, my fists clenched, imagining what I'd do if one of Meg's friends turned up at our door, upset and crying. Would I make her go back? Call her parents? Or would I call the police? I'm wondering what Meg's been saying to make Karen think she's unhappy. *Is* she unhappy? I choke back a sob, the fight leaving me. I pick up my chair and sit down. 'When did she get here?' I ask quietly.

'About five o'clock,' Karen says. She looks at PC Clarke, who nods for her to continue. 'She took the train here, and she was hungry and cold. I gave her something to eat. At first I thought you knew she was here, and when I found out you didn't, I said we must ring you, but she made me promise not to.'

'You should have called anyway,' I mutter. I feel Steve's hand on my arm again.

'The thing is,' Karen says, 'I was scared that if I broke that promise she wouldn't trust me again. And then where would she go, the next time she needed a shoulder to cry on?'

To me, I want to say. *To her mum.* But I don't say it, because doesn't Karen have a point? Isn't it better that Meg came here, to this warm, safe house, rather than wandering the streets? I look at Karen, her face filled with compassion for my daughter – for all of us – and I know that I'm not angry with Karen. I'm angry with myself. For not being good enough, for not being what Meg needed, for hurting her with my words.

'Thank you,' I say now. 'Thank you for looking after Meg.'

Karen reaches across the table and squeezes my hand. 'How could I not?' *How could I not, when my son's heart beats in her chest*, she means, and a shiver runs through me. I can't shake the feeling that, by giving up Jake's heart, Karen is laying claim on my daughter.

I think of the fairy tale about the woodcutter and his wife, bargaining with the witch for the food they need to survive. *I'll give you the food*, she tells them. *But you must give me your first-born child* . . . In despair, the woodcutter agrees. Years pass, and the promise is forgotten . . .

Until their baby is born.

I shake myself. *Stop it, Lizzie.* I make myself smile at Karen, and then we all jump as there's a noise on the stairs, and Meg appears in the kitchen. She looks worried – she thinks Steve and me are going to give her a row – and she pulls her school jumper over her hands, stretching the arms.

'Hi, Mum. Hi, Dad.' The greeting is quiet and flat.

Karen coughs. 'And . . .' She's prompting Meg, I realise, as my daughter looks at Karen and gives a small nod.

'I'm sorry I didn't come home. I'm sorry I worried you.'

I go to her and wrap her in my arms, relief making me cry. Steve joins me, and we stand in a huddle so tight I don't know where Meg finishes and Steve begins. 'I'm so sorry,' I say, my voice breaking. Meg's crying too, and I hold her close until I hear a cough from one of the police officers. Reluctantly, I pull away.

'Do you need . . .' I point vaguely at the police officers' notebooks. There must be paperwork, I suppose, when a missing child is found.

'We've got everything we need, thank you.' PC Clarke looks at Meg sternly. 'Don't go worrying your parents like that again please, young lady.'

I put an arm round Meg's shoulders, suddenly protective of her. 'Come on, love, time to get you home.' She says something so quietly I can barely hear it.

That can't be right – can it?

'What did you say, love?'

'I said no.' Meg looks at her feet. 'I don't want to go home. I want to stay with Karen.'

Chapter 7

The Break-Up

I stare at Meg, confused and speechless. Steve finds the words before I do, exploding in a bark of disbelief.

'Don't be ridiculous, Meg, you're coming home.'

'But I want to stay here.' She looks at Karen. 'Please. Just for a few days.'

A wave of anger builds inside me and I cross the room to where Karen is sitting, her face all innocent, as if she had nothing to do with this. 'What have you been saying to her?'

'Nothing, Lizzie, this is as much a surprise to me as it is to—'

'Liar!' I scream at her. She doesn't react, which somehow makes me even more angry. Before I know what I'm doing, my arm has left my side and my hand snaps through the air and onto Karen's face. It makes a sound like a cracking whip. Instantly, a mark appears on her cheek, the curve of my fingertips marked out in red.

'Lizzie!' Steve sounds as shocked as I feel. I have never hit anyone before, never lost my temper so badly that I lost control. I take a step back, just as the two police officers move to stand between me and Karen.

'What the hell, Mum?'

'Are you okay?' I hear PC Stanford ask Karen. 'Let's get some ice on that, shall we?' Meg rushes to the fridge, where there's an ice-dispenser, and wraps some in a tea towel. She moves around the kitchen like she already lives here.

'Mrs Thomas,' PC Clarke says, and her voice is harder now than when I was the mother of a missing child. 'I understand emotions are running high, but there's no excuse for violence. Mrs Edwards is well within her rights to press charges for assault.'

My pulse races, blood singing in my ears. What have I done? I imagine being carted out in hand-cuffs, placed in a cell, charged and taken to court. I might lose my job, and what would we do then?

'I won't be pressing charges,' Karen says. 'Lizzie was upset – I quite understand.'

'I'm so sorry,' Steve says, and I know that should be my line, but I can't speak. I'm frozen to the spot, horrified by what I've done.

'Let's just forget it, shall we?' Karen takes the ice

pack away from her cheek. The skin is a violent red, and I hear Meg gasp.

'It's very good of you,' Steve says. He looks at me. 'Isn't it, Lizzie?'

'Y – yes,' I manage. 'Thank you, Karen. And I really am sorry – I just . . .'

I just hate you, I finish silently. *And I wish you'd never come into our lives.*

Except that without Karen – without her son Jake – Meg wouldn't be standing here now.

I turn to my daughter. 'Why don't you want to come home, Meg? What is it we've done?' I feel the police officers' eyes burning into me, accusing me of unspoken crimes. Do they think we beat her? Worse?

'Nothing.' Meg speaks firmly. 'You and Dad are amazing. The best parents anyone could ever have.' The band around my chest eases slightly. Meg looks up at me, her face far wiser than her years. 'I'm finding it really hard, Mum. Knowing I wouldn't be here if Jake hadn't lived – finding out all the things he liked, that suddenly I like too . . .' She trails off, searching for the words. 'I want to know more about him – to live a tiny bit of his life, so that he's a real person in my head, not just something beating in my chest.' She gives a hollow laugh. 'It doesn't make any sense, I know.'

It doesn't. And yet I remember a programme Steve and I watched on TV, about a couple who adopted a baby from China. He wasn't even a year old when he left – no memory of his parents, or where he used to live – but his adoptive mum and dad took him back every few years, cooked Chinese food, sent him to Mandarin Chinese lessons . . . *It's part of who he is*, I remember them saying.

'I understand,' I tell Meg. I look at Karen, her cheek still raw and swollen.

'Meg's welcome to stay, of course, but I don't want to cause—'

'It's fine,' I say curtly.

'It's fine,' Steve echoes. The police officers are looking at each of us in turn, trying to work out what's going on. PC Clarke sighs.

'Let me get this straight. Meg, you'd like to stay here instead of going home?'

'Yes, please.'

'And Mrs Edwards, you're happy to have her?'

'Absolutely.'

'And Mr and Mrs Thomas, you're happy to let her?'

'Well, I wouldn't say *happy*—' I start, but Steve talks over me.

'Yes.' He's not smiling. A muscle is twitching in his cheek, the way it does when he's angry.

But it isn't Karen – or even Meg – he's angry with.

'This is all your fault,' he says, when we're in the car, with the gravel on Karen's drive crunching beneath our wheels. 'You drove her away.'

'That isn't true. She said we were amazing parents – you heard her!'

'The way you've been about Karen . . . it's no wonder Meg doesn't want to be under the same roof as you. As for tonight – I've never seen anything like it. That poor woman's face!'

He moves out when we get home. Packs a bag and says he *needs some time to think*. And I sit in the kitchen with a bottle of wine and wonder how I lost a daughter and a husband in the space of a few hours. Where did it all go wrong?

When we met Karen.

The thought is there before I can stop it, and for the first time I listen to it properly, not pushing it away. We were fine before I got the letter from Karen. Steve and I were happy. Meg was settled. This is all Karen's fault. I think about what Samira said – that getting in touch with donor families was asking for trouble – and I realise she was right. I should never have replied to Karen's letter, never have agreed to let her meet Meg. Now it's too late.

*

The days are empty without Meg to look after, and I take on extra shifts at the factory. I text Steve, begging him to come home, but get a terse *staying with Dan – need to get my head together* in response.

Meg's messages to me are more forgiving.

Love you Mum x

Don't worry – I'm doing my homework! x

Karen's taking me to the theatre tonight!!! X

I stare at this last message, its extra exclamation marks showing how excited my daughter is. She has been to the theatre before. We took her to the panto when she was seven, and again a few years later. But perhaps she doesn't remember. Perhaps panto doesn't count. I imagine Karen helping Meg get ready. I see them rifle through the small bag of clothes Steve took round to Karen's the day after we left Meg there. Maybe Karen wrinkled her nose – said *oh no, this won't do at all* – and took Meg shopping for something more suitable. What do people like Karen wear to the theatre? I look down at my jeans and fleece, and think it's no wonder Meg chose to be with Karen instead of frumpy old Mum.

Samira drops by on her way to work, narrowing her eyes at my tear-stained face. 'What's happened?'

'Steve's moved out.' That, at least, I can tell her. 'Why?'

That, I can't. 'He says he needs time to think. We've been having a few problems.' To put it mildly.

'Is Meg okay?'

'She seems very . . . happy.' It sticks in my throat.

Samira looks worried. 'It's not unusual for couples to have problems after a transplant. I can give you details of some counselling services if that would help?'

'Thanks,' I say. Anything to avoid telling the truth. 'That would be great.' I paste a smile on my face, but Samira looks at me thoughtfully.

'Is there something you're not telling me, Lizzie?'

I so badly want to tell her. I want to let it all spill out, and have her tell me what to do – how to handle it. But I can't. So I shake my head and say *no, nothing at all*, and make excuses for why I can't invite her in for a cuppa.

At the weekend, four days after we left Meg at Karen's house, she comes home. I hear the key in the lock and run down the stairs, and as she steps through the door I wrap my daughter in my arms.

'Meggie, I've missed you so much.'

She pulls away, and I realise she didn't come alone.

'Hi, Lizzie.' Karen's voice is sweet, as though

nothing happened between us. As though I never slapped her. As though she wasn't trying to turn my daughter against me.

'Karen.'

She nudges Meg. 'Don't you have something to say to Mum?'

I don't know what's more irritating: the way she's behaving like Meg's mother, or the way she said 'Mum', like we're all part of the same happy family.

Meg flushes, and looks at the floor. 'I'm sorry I ran away, and I'm sorry I upset you by not coming home.' It sounds as if she has practised saying this, and I imagine Karen coaching her on the way over here.

'That's okay, sweetheart,' I say, a million times more cheerfully than I feel. 'Say goodbye to Karen, and thank her for having you.' I'm being rude, not inviting Karen to come in, but I don't care. I've already decided: we won't be seeing any more of her – not if I can help it.

Meg throws her arms around Karen. 'Thanks a million – I had the best time.' They stand like that for a second, embracing. And I look at the ceiling, at the window – anywhere but at my daughter. She is acting as if she never wants to be parted from this woman we've known for five seconds. Only I can't help myself and, when I look back,

61

Karen has her hands on my daughter's cheeks, holding Meg's face close to her own.

'Remember what we talked about, hmm?' Karen whispers. It's an intimate moment and I feel awkward to be watching them.

'I know,' Meg says. 'And I will, I promise.' She takes one of Karen's hands and presses it briefly to her heart, and I clench my fists by my side.

'Bye, then,' I say. Karen looks surprised by my bluntness, but is too polite to say anything. She kisses Meg again – *enough, already!* – and says goodbye.

'How was the theatre?' I ask Meg.

'Amazing!' Meg's eyes shine. 'We should go. Karen says you can get season tickets.'

Bully for Karen, I think, wondering a) whether a theatre season ticket is more than a football season ticket, and b) if Steve could ever be persuaded to give up his beloved Arsenal games.

'Is Dad at work?' Meg asks. I look at the clock, stalling for time. Actually, he is . . . but I'm going to have to tell her sometime.

'Sweetheart, Dad's gone away for a few days.'

The alarm on Meg's face is instant. 'You've split up, haven't you? Is it because of me?' Tears form in the corners of her eyes.

'No! He's just staying at Dan's for a bit. Like you stayed at Karen's.' *Just without the theatre tickets and the shopping trips*, I think. Meg looks doubtful, and I mentally cross my fingers. 'There's nothing wrong, sweetheart, I promise.'

I wait till Meg is asleep before I call Steve to tell him she's home.

'I know,' he said. 'Karen told me.' Resentment seeps through me. Did she text him? Call? Or did they meet up to share a bottle of wine, Karen moving a little closer to my husband with each sip?

'Now she's back,' I say, 'are you coming home?' The pause that follows gives me Steve's answer before he even speaks.

'I need to think about stuff,' he says. 'Lizzie – the way you were at Karen's . . . it's a side to you I've never seen before – never even knew existed.'

'I lost my temper. It won't happen again.'

'It isn't just that, though. Karen's lost her whole family – she's all alone – but you don't seem to care. You used to be so kind, and now . . . I don't know who you are any more, Lizzie.' He puts down the phone. I'm left listening to my own heartbeat, as I press the silent receiver to my ear. A mix of grief and anger swirls in my stomach.

Karen may have lost her family, but she's not having mine.

Chapter 8

Looking for Answers

'I don't want you seeing Karen again,' I tell Meg, the next day. We're eating breakfast, the empty place at the table a constant reminder of Steve's absence. Meg's been quiet and withdrawn ever since she came home, hunched over her phone texting someone she won't let me see.

'What?' Meg's spoon clatters into her cereal bowl, milk splashing onto the table. 'Why?'

Because she's trying to take you away from me, I think. 'I don't think it's good for her,' I say instead. I was awake all night thinking of the best way to approach this. I feel guilty, pretending it's Karen I care about, but I think it's the only way to get through to Meg. 'She's been through a terrible trauma,' I tell Meg, whose mouth is still open in outrage. 'She needs to grieve for Jake and his dad – I don't think it's healthy for her to focus all her attention on you. She's . . .' I think of a word I read once in a magazine.

'Projecting,' I say, the strange word clumsy on my lips.

'She's what?'

'Projecting. Moving the feelings she has for her son, to you. It's not healthy.' *For either of you*, I want to add. I see the hurt in my daughter's eyes, and waver a fraction.

You're doing the right thing, I remind myself. I need to put things back the way they were before Karen came on the scene. She and Jake did a wonderful thing for Meg, and we will always be grateful, but that doesn't earn Karen a place in our lives. I don't want her here.

What about what Meg wants? a voice in my head says.

'Karen says I'm the only good thing to come out of all the sadness,' Meg says. She looks at me, her eyes pleading. 'She needs me, Mum, and . . .' she pauses, and even before she finishes her sentence I know it's going to hurt. 'I need her.'

'You've already got a family, Meg!' It's out before I can stop it, and Meg's eyes narrow.

'This isn't about what's healthy for Karen at all, is it? You're jealous! My God, Mum, you're jealous of a woman who lost her whole family!' She shakes her head, and the disgust on her face makes me cry inside, but I can't deny it. It's true. I *am* jealous of Karen, and of the closeness I saw between her and

65

Meg. And of the respect I see in Steve's eyes when he talks about her. Jealous of a grieving mother – what kind of horrible person does that make me?

Meg pushes back her chair. 'I'm going to my room.'

'You haven't finished your breakfast.'

'I'm not hungry any more.' She stomps out of the room, slamming the door behind her.

What a mess I've made of all this. All I want to do is protect my family – that's all I've ever tried to do – but instead I've driven them away.

I try to distract myself with housework, clearing out the kitchen cupboards and pulling the sofa from the wall to hoover behind it. But all the time I see Karen Edwards in my head. I need to show Steve and Meg that Karen isn't the perfect woman they think she is. Somehow I need to make them understand that all my instincts are screaming at me to stay away from this woman. But how do I do that, when she's done nothing wrong?

I get out my laptop and log on. I don't even know what I'm hoping to see, but I have to do something.

Karen isn't hard to find. Google brings up dozens of news sites about the tragic crash that ended the life of her husband, Michael, and their seventeen-year-old son, Jake.

Karen and Michael had given Jake the motorbike for his birthday, a few weeks before. 'If only we'd got him a PlayStation instead,' Karen is quoted as saying. 'A laptop – anything but that bike.' The quote runs with a picture of a distressed Karen in her lounge, holding a family photo. Despite my feelings about her, I feel a lump in my throat.

I scan the articles. I learn that Karen's husband was the biker, and that Jake had been obsessed with them from a young age as a result. Karen refused even to sit on a bike. I learn that the accident was no one's fault; an icy road, poor visibility, a new rider. Jake had lost control, skidding into his dad. Michael Edwards died at the scene; Jake a few hours later at the hospital, his mother by his side.

The doctors would have had the conversation as Jake was dying. *Mrs Edwards, I know this is the worst possible time to ask you to make decisions . . .* They would have talked about organ donation, about the lives Jake could save. Whichever organs had survived the accident and were suitable for transplant; his eyes, his kidneys, his liver . . . and of course, his heart.

I stare at the photo of Jake. He's standing beside a bike with a helium balloon tied to the handlebars. *Happy Birthday!* He's wearing jeans and a hoodie, with Converse trainers and a bunch of leather bracelets tied round his wrist. He's grinning from ear to ear – obviously chuffed to bits with his present. He looks like a nice kid.

I swallow hard. What am I doing? I imagine what it would be like if it were the other way round – if Meg had died instead of Jake. I imagine how empty our lives would be. And I imagine how much it would mean to me, to know that Meg's death had saved someone else from the heartache I was feeling. I'm sobbing hard when I pick up the phone and dial Samira's number.

'Hiya Lizzie, y'all right? I'm about to go into the ward – can I ring you later?'

'Okay,' I say, but I can't hide the gulp that follows, and there's a change in Samira's tone.

'What's wrong? Is it Meg? Shall I call—'

'No – no, Meg's fine,' I reassure her. 'But . . . Samira, I've done something stupid.' Silence fills the phone line, and I picture Samira, standing outside the hospital, worried she'll be late for work. I speak quickly. 'I've been talking to the mother of Meg's donor. I know – I know! I ignored your advice. And I'm not handling it well, Samira. Meg adores her, and they're spending so much time together, and – I'm not proud of this – it's making me feel like an outsider.'

Samira sighs. 'I did warn you, Lizzie. Look, I hate to do this, but I'm going to be late if—'

68

But now that I'm confessing, I can't stop. 'I googled them,' I tell Samira, 'and I'm the one with the problem – not them. They look like a nice family. He got a bike for his seventeenth birthday and was killed out on the road with his dad a few days later – it must have been awful.'

'Um, Lizzie . . .'

'I saw photos of him – he was just a boy, Samira! Why am I finding this so hard to—'

'Lizzie!' Samira's shout stuns me into silence. 'Listen to me. I have to go into work, but I'm going to call you the second I get a break, okay? You've got the wrong end of the stick.'

'What do you mean?'

'I shouldn't even be telling you this, you know that . . .' Samira sighs. 'But Meg's donor wasn't a seventeen-year-old boy. He was a thirty-five-year-old man. Don't do anything, okay, Lizzie? I'll call you the second I can.'

The line goes dead and I hold the silent phone to my ear, my heart pounding. Jake wasn't Meg's donor?

Then who the hell is Karen Edwards, and what does she want with my family?

Chapter 9

Missing

'Meg!' I shout up the stairs, taking a step towards the hall. Then I turn back, so thrown by what I've just learned, that I don't know where I am. What should I do? Who is Karen Edwards? My fingers hover over the keys on my phone. 'Meg!'

I'm trying to make sense of what I've just found out. I saw the newspaper reports. The accident was just as Karen said it was – she told us the truth.

Except for one important detail. Meg's heart didn't belong to Jake Edwards.

Who do I call first: Steve, or the police? Or should I go to the station in person? That would be better – they won't be able to fob me off if I'm standing in front of them. 'Meg!' I call her again. She'll have to come with me – I'm not letting her out of my sight again.

The police will want the letter Karen sent – the letter that started all this. Where is it? My breath is coming in bursts, fast and shallow, making me light-headed. I stop for a second, place my hands flat on the kitchen table to ground myself.

'Calm down,' I say out loud. I might not know who Karen really is, or what she wants, but at least I've uncovered her lies before anything terrible happened. Or have I? My chest tightens at the thought of the days Meg spent at Karen's house. I assumed Meg was angry with me for butting in, but what if something dreadful happened at Karen's house?

I stop myself. No, Meg's obsessed with Karen – that's part of the problem. That's why she wouldn't believe me when I said something wasn't right. Well, she'll have to believe me now. I take the stairs two at a time and burst into Meg's room without knocking.

'Meg, this is going to come as a bit of a shock . . .' I look around Meg's tiny room. Is she in the loo? I step onto the landing, but the door to the bathroom we all share is wide open – there's no one inside. 'Meg?' I say. And then I see it: her bedroom window, wide open, the photos and trinkets on her windowsill pushed to one side. Meg's gone.

My mobile is still in my hand, and this time I don't hesitate. I call 999, leaning out of the window as I talk to the operator. Meg's bedroom is above the kitchen, a flat-roofed extension put on by the people who lived here before us. By the back door is a bench, easing Meg's drop down to the patio. Did she go when I was on the phone to Samira? Or sooner, when the hoover was on and I wouldn't have heard her window open? I look at my watch. Meg came up to her room at breakfast time and it's almost midday now – she's been gone for hours.

'I see this is the second time your daughter's been reported missing in the last two weeks,' the police operator says.

'Yes, but—'

'And she was found safe and well at a friend's house, is that right?'

'Not a friend!' I say angrily. 'She's been lying to us!' I stumble through the whole story, but it sounds insane. Even though the operator tells me the police are on their way to Karen's house, I call Steve.

'The police want me to stay here, in case Meg comes back,' I tell him, once I've told him every-thing. 'They need to take another report.'

'I'll go to Karen's,' he says, without hesitation. A wave of relief washes over me. He believes me. We might have our differences, but when I need him, he's there. For me, and for Meg.

Waiting is agony. The police arrive – the same pair as last time – and they fill out the forms, asking all the same questions as last time.

'You know all this!' I say, frustrated. 'Shouldn't you be at –' I can't bring myself to say her name, '– *that woman's* house instead?'

'Officers are on their way to her address,' says PC Clarke. 'They'll call the second they have an update.' As if on cue, her radio crackles into life. 'Excuse me,' she says, going into the garden to take the call. I watch through the window, trying to interpret her expression.

'I'm sorry,' she says, when she returns. 'There's no one at Mrs Edwards' house. Is there anywhere else you think she might have gone?'

'Meg's with Karen, I just know it.'

'We'll send out a description,' PC Stanford says, 'and if you could contact Meg's other friends, that would be great. In the meantime, what can you tell us about Karen Edwards?'

I realise that, for all the chats I've had with Karen – or about her, with Meg – I know hardly anything about her. Not where she works, or who her friends are, or where she might be now, with my daughter.

'Only that she's been lying to us for weeks,' I say bitterly.

'Can you think of any reason why she'd want to pretend to be the mother of Meg's donor?' PC Clarke says.

'She's mad,' I say. She must be, to do something

73

so sick, something so strange. Just then my mobile rings, Steve's name flashing up on the screen. I snatch it up. 'Have you found her?'

'I've been knocking on doors in the street,' Steve says. He sounds like I feel – wrung-out and sick with worry. 'One of the neighbours saw them together an hour ago, outside Karen's house.'

'And Meg was okay? She wasn't hurt?'

PC Clarke raises an eyebrow. I mouth *someone saw Meg* at her.

'Yes, but . . .' Steve's voice breaks. 'They were getting into a car. They had suitcases with them, Lizzie – the neighbour said it looked like they were going away for a while.'

There's a buzzing in my ears and I think I might be about to faint. Numbly, I pass the mobile to PC Clarke, who takes over with a brisk air of authority. I stumble out of the kitchen and into the hall, clutching at the bannister as I go upstairs and into Meg's bedroom again. I have to check something. I have to know if my instincts are right, yet again . . .

In the bottom of Meg's wardrobe is a bag she took on a school trip to France that we saved all year to pay for. Afterwards she put everything – her travel pillow, an adaptor, even some left-over Euros – in the case and zipped it shut. 'Ready for next time,' she told me, as if we're the sort of family who have a holiday every year. I unzip the case. The pillow is there, the adaptor, the money . . . but my instincts were right. Meg's passport is missing. Karen is taking her out of the country.

Chapter 10

A Race Against Time

I've never been in a police station before. Never even had to call the police before this month, and now I feel like I've always been here – that PCs Clarke and Stanford have always been with us. We drove in convoy to the station. Steve followed the police car, his knuckles white on the steering wheel, me in the passenger seat, unable to stop crying.

'They'll find her, love,' Steve kept saying. But I couldn't stop my mind going to dark places that made the tears come even harder. When I thought Meg had Jake's heart, I could understand Karen's obsession with her. I didn't like it, but I understood it. Meg had a piece of her son – it made sense that Karen was deeply attached. But Karen has nothing to do with the heart that saved Meg's life, so what does she want from us? Why did she lie to us?

We parked the car and followed PC Clarke to the room we're in now. It's stuffy and too hot, the thermostat turned up to tropical. There's a table and four chairs, and lots of detectives who come in and out, asking questions and writing in small black notebooks. *Who was Meg's consultant? What's Samira's last name? What medication does Meg take? Did Karen ever mention any other locations – anywhere abroad?*

The door opens, and Detective Sergeant Morgan comes in. She's in charge, I think – at least, that's the impression she gives. But there are so many officers, and so many questions, and it all seems to be moving so fast, yet at the same time far, far too slowly.

'Another cup of tea?' DS Morgan nods towards PC Stanford, who hurries out of the room, presumably to make it. I don't remember drinking the last one.

'Is there news?' I try to read the detective sergeant's face, but she's played this game more times than I have.

'There's nothing in our files for Karen Edwards.' DS Morgan skirts my question. 'She has no criminal record. She isn't listed with social services, or on the sex offender's register.'

'Maybe she's just never been caught,' Steve says grimly. I let out a cry. My poor baby.

'There's a black Audi registered in her name – index number AKE 340 – which I believe fits with

77

what you've seen her driving?' I nod. 'We've logged the number with ANPR – that's automatic number plate recognition – so if she passes any cameras we'll get a hit and know what direction she's travelling in.'

'She told Meg to bring her passport,' I say. 'Are you checking the airports?' There are three within striking distance.

'We've issued an alert to all airports, as well as ferry ports.' DS Morgan says. 'But they might not be going abroad – Karen might have wanted Meg's passport for some other reason. ID for new documents, for example.'

'Why is she doing this?' My words come out in a wail, and Steve squeezes my hand.

'Has Karen ever asked you for money?' DS Morgan says. 'It's a common reason for kidnap and—'

I laugh – a hard bark too loud for the room. 'She's backing the wrong horse if she thinks she can get money out of us – we're barely scraping by ourselves.'

'Is that what you think this is about?' Steve says. 'Because if she wants money, we'll get it somehow. We'll speak to the bank – get another mortgage. Anything to get Meg back.' He's close to tears, his words choking in his throat.

'There's no sign of a ransom demand at the

moment,' DC Morgan says. 'Did your daughter know Jake Edwards? They were only a few years apart – could Karen be taking revenge for something Meg did or said?'

I feel Steve stiffen at the suggestion. 'Meg wouldn't hurt a fly,' I say. 'Besides, she didn't know Jake. We don't even live in the same area as them.'

'We'll look into possible connections anyway,' DS Morgan says. 'After school clubs, friends of friends – that sort of thing.' I slump into my chair. This is hopeless. They don't have any solid leads, they're just fumbling in the dark.

'One other thing.' DS Morgan hesitates, and I sit up, my nerve-endings tingling. Something's happened. Something bad. 'You mentioned that Meg has to take medication.'

I nod. 'They stop her body rejecting the heart. She has to take them every day.'

'How much of the drug do you have?'

'Six weeks' worth,' I say. 'Divided into two pots. Meg keeps one in her room – she's really good about taking them – and the other one's in the bathroom cabinet. When Meg's is empty I give her the reserve pot, and order the repeat prescription.' I look around the room, confused as to why they're asking. 'Meg took her pot with her when she left – I've checked.'

'We got a warrant to search Karen's house for

evidence,' DS Morgan says. 'In the bin in the kitchen we found Meg's medication.'

My blood runs cold. Without the drugs Meg's body will start fighting the transplanted heart, seeing it as the enemy. How long will it take before her breath starts to catch? Before her arms and legs ache when she moves, and she grows pale and listless? There's only one reason why Karen would throw away Meg's medication. She wants her to die.

But why?

The next half hour passes in a blur. The police found Meg's mobile at Karen's house, too. They passed it to me in a clear plastic bag so I could enter her password. Reading the WhatsApp conversation between Meg and Karen was agony.

Mum's trying to stop me seeing you. I hate her.

She can't stop you – you're almost an adult. Do you want me to pick you up?

Yes please xxx

'I thought I was doing the right thing,' I cry, 'stopping her from seeing Karen, but I made things worse!' Steve puts his arm around me, just as the door opens and PC Stanford comes in, followed by a familiar face.

'Samira!' I jump up and hug her, sobbing into her uniform. Then DS Morgan pulls up another chair to the table. Samira looks as worried as Steve and I are, her eyes red-rimmed from crying. PC Stanford addresses DS Morgan.

'This is Samira Kaur,' she says. 'She's the nurse who looked after Meg after her transplant, and is a good friend of the family's now. She has an update on Karen Edwards.'

Everyone's eyes swivel to Samira, and we all hold our breaths for what she's about to tell us. Samira swallows.

'We don't tell patients who their organs come from,' she says, 'and we advise them strongly not to try to get in touch themselves. It can cause all sorts of problems for both sides.' I flush, although she isn't directing this at me. 'Meg's heart came from a thirty-five-year-old man with kidney failure. His heart was healthy, and a good match for Meg, and the transplant was a success.'

I start to feel impatient. We know all this. Why is Samira here? What has she found out?

'Lizzie told me Karen and Jake's names, and I looked them up on the hospital system. It's just as the newspaper articles said: Jake and his dad had a bike accident, and his dad died at the scene. Jake was rushed to hospital and for a while it looked like he might have made it. Only . . .' her eyes glisten. 'Only his heart gave up. The doctor treating him says he did everything he could. He said Jake's mum begged him not to give up.'

I picture Karen at the hospital, her son dying in theatre. And a doctor, breaking the news, telling Karen that Jake's heart is failing. Slowly, the pieces of the puzzle fall into place.

'Karen thought Jake should have had the heart that went to Meg,' I say, and it isn't really a question, because it suddenly seems so obvious.

Samira nods. 'Jake and Meg were in surgery at the same time. It seems Karen overheard one of the doctors talking about the donor, and Karen begged him to give the heart to Jake.'

I see the scene as vividly as if it was playing out in front of me and, despite everything, I feel a pang of grief for Karen. What must that have been like? Knowing your son was dying? Begging that doctor for what you thought was the answer?

'Jake was critically injured,' Samira says. 'There were lots of reasons why he wasn't suitable for a transplant, but Karen was fixated. As far as she was concerned, that heart would have saved Jake's life.'

'And Meg got it,' I say, almost to myself. *That poor woman*, I find myself thinking, before everything snaps back and my heart hardens again. *That poor woman* has abducted my daughter, and she intends to harm her. 'You have to find her,' I say to DS Morgan, my voice rising with each word. 'You have to find her now!'

As if I've made it happen, DS Morgan's mobile rings, and she answers it with a curt, 'Morgan.' She nods to the unseen speaker, saying 'what time was that?' and 'understood'. She finishes the call and turns to the uniformed officers, a new urgency in her voice. 'Confirmed sighting,' she says. 'Heathrow, terminal three. I want everyone we've got there. Go!'

There's a flurry of uniform and banging doors, and running feet in the corridor outside. I hear sirens and shouts, and my heart thuds in my chest like it's going to break out. I stand up, pulling Steve with me. 'We have to go.'

DS Morgan stands too, her hands out in an attempt to calm me. 'Let us do our job, Mrs Thomas. The best thing you can do is stay here and—'

But I'm not listening. I'm pushing past her, and Steve's following, and we're running from the room and out of the station to the car. We're going to get our daughter back.

Chapter 11

Face to Face

They were too late, we heard, as we ran to the car. Snatches of radio, of updates from one officer to another. The block on the passport came too late – Karen had already checked them both in online. They won't show their passports till they're at the gate. They'll be stopped then – they won't be allowed on the plane – but for now they are missing. Somewhere in the departure area, among the shops and the bars and the business lounges.

We drive in silence, the sirens leading the way and then fading as we fall behind, unable to keep up with the police cars' blue flashing lights. I stare out of the window, praying that Karen won't hurt Meg, that Meg isn't frightened. Steve's jaw is rigid, a muscle twitching in his cheek.

'Karen had everything,' he says eventually, almost as though he's talking to himself. 'Big house, nice car, expensive clothes, a good education.' I stay silent. 'I thought she'd be a good influence on Meg, you know? I figured it was good for Meg to see what she could achieve if she worked hard.'

'We couldn't have known.'

'You knew.' He glances at me. 'And I wouldn't listen. I put Meg at risk – I encouraged her to keep seeing Karen.'

I close my eyes, willing the miles to pass, wishing I could hear the police talk to each other on the radio. Maybe they're there, now. Maybe airport officials have already found them. Maybe they've sat Meg down with a cup of sweet tea and told her she's *safe now, nothing to worry about.*

Or maybe, a voice in my head whispers, maybe Karen's too clever for that. Maybe she has fake ID, maybe she doesn't care about the flight to Spain – after all, if you're going to kill a child does it matter where you do it? I let out a strangled sob, and Steve lifts his hand from the gear stick to put over mine.

'Nearly there,' he says.

We abandon the car on double yellow lines, ignoring the shouts of the ticket warden, and running into the terminal. I've never been abroad, and I think back to Meg's excited chatter on her return from France. She told us about the security queue, about taking off her belt, and emptying her bag of electronics and liquids. I scan the building,

85

and am dismayed to see the uniformed man at the entrance to the security area. He is scanning pieces of paper presented by each traveller.

'We won't get through!' I say to Steve. 'Look!'

'Come on,' he says grimly. He'll never forgive himself for trusting Karen, I know, and yet I don't blame him. Steve's right – she *does* have everything. A big house, a nice car, great clothes . . . But not Meg. She's not having our Meg.

I follow Steve towards security, half-running to keep up with his long strides. As we approach he mutters to me, 'I'll distract him – you slip past,' and my pulse thumps in my ears. *Slip past?* I can't! They'll see – they'll stop me.

The security man is big and burly, arms straining at his sleeves. Steve gives my hand a final squeeze then drops it, moving a few paces in front of me, his eyes fixed on the guard. 'Excuse me!' he calls.

I try to breathe deeply. Surely everyone can see the heat rising through my body? The sweat breaking out across my brow?

Come on, Lizzie, I tell myself. *What's the worst that can happen?*

Meg getting hurt, comes the answer. Nothing else matters. My breathing slows, and I hold my head up. Steve breaks into a jog and grabs the security man around the shoulders, saying *Please*

86

help me, my daughter's missing. I slip past them both and join the mercifully short queue for security.

Unsure exactly what they need, I throw my handbag and the contents of my pockets into a black tray.

'Shoes,' says a bored girl with a tight, high ponytail.

'What?' Panic rises in my throat. *Meg. I need to get to Meg.*

'You have to take your shoes off.'

Frustrated, I tear off my shoes, and walk through the archway, crossing my fingers that nothing else will hold me up. And it doesn't, and I'm through, abandoning my handbag and running, running, running with no idea of where she might be, only that she's here somewhere. My Meg.

I'm close to tears, my breath short and painful as I run barefoot into every shop, every restaurant, looking wildly around for Karen and my daughter. People look at me, amused, pointing and nudging each other. I don't care.

'Have you seen a fourteen-year-old girl?' I say. I reach for my phone to find a picture, then remember it's on a conveyor belt with my handbag. With my shoes. There are shrugs and head-shakes – awkward glances as though I might be mad.

I hear the commotion before I see it. Confident

commands of *get back please*, and *nothing to see here*. I break into a run and follow the noise, my feet pounding the floor in time to the voice in my head: *Meg, Meg, Meg.*

Around the disabled toilet between two gates is a crowd of people, straining their necks to see to the front. I push through them, to where sunhats and shorts give way to police hats and dark blue trousers.

'Stay back, please, madam.' A police officer with a large black moustache holds up a hand. 'All of you,' he raises his voice, shouting at the crowd. 'Back off!' There's a grumble as people start to amble away, moved on by seemingly dozens of uniformed staff.

'They're in there, aren't they?' I say. 'Meg and Karen?'

There's a moment's hesitation. 'I can't release any information about—'

'She's my daughter!' I scream it long and loud, the tears finally coming, so fast I wonder if they'll ever stop. Alarm shows on his face, and he grips my shoulder, half in support and half in restraint. He beckons to an officer standing by the toilet door. He comes over, his look of annoyance turning to concern once moustache-man tells him who I am.

'Everything's under control,' he says. 'I'll have

someone escort you to one of the offices, where you can wait for updates.'

'I'm going nowhere,' I tell him. 'Not till I see my daughter.'

'We're waiting for a negotiator, Mrs Thomas.'

'A what?' I don't even hear the word, let alone understand it. The crowd has been moved back now, this entire section cleared of anyone but airport staff, police, and me. And Karen and Meg, presumably locked in the toilet.

'Someone trained in talking to people,' the police officer explains. 'The negotiator will help Mrs Edwards understand that her best option is to come out quietly.'

'Come out?' Frustration boils inside me. 'Why are you waiting for her to come out? Just bash the door in – isn't that what you lot do?'

And then I take in the kindness in the officer's eyes, the emptied section of the airport, the sheer number of police summoned for one woman and a schoolgirl. And I understand.

'She said she'll hurt Meg if you open the door, didn't she?'

There's a pause, then the officer nods. 'It took a while to locate Edwards on CCTV, but when we did, she dragged your daughter into this washroom.'

I think of the security queue, of the liquids and handbags emptied onto the conveyor belt. 'She

89

can't have a weapon though, can she? Not here? She can't hurt Meg.' I don't know if I'm asking the question, or pleading for that to be true.

'We have nothing to suggest that Edwards is armed,' the police officer says. 'But . . .' his voice is gentle. Kind. 'It's possible to hurt someone without weapons, Mrs Thomas.'

My heart contracts. Meg is right there. *Right there*. Ten metres from me, yet I can't keep her safe. I push past the police officer, hammer on the locked door and scream Meg's name, so she knows she's not alone. Behind me I hear someone – a police officer? – swear. Someone else grabs my shoulder and pulls me back, but then there's a hard click and the door flies open with a slam against the wall.

'Meg!' I cry.

'Mum!'

Karen's hand is twisted into Meg's hair, pulling her head backwards. In her free hand is a jagged piece from a glass bottle, the sharp point pushed against Meg's exposed neck. Karen looks at me, a twisted smile on her face.

'Finally,' she says. 'I've been waiting for you.'

Chapter 12

Taken Hostage

The glass is green. It shimmers in the light like something magical – something from a fairy tale. I think again of the woodcutter fable. *You must give me your first-born child . . .*

'Let her go,' I say, my voice shaky. 'Please, Karen, just let her go.'

'Mum, I'm scared.' Tears run down the sides of Meg's face.

'It's okay, love, it's going to be all right.' I don't know if it's true, but I have to believe it. Meg is my world, my everything.

'Jake died because of her,' Karen says. As she speaks, she twists the glass in her hand. Meg cries out, and a thin trickle of blood runs down her pale neck. I feel the pain as keenly as if the glass were in my own neck.

'Let go of my daughter!' I roar. I step forward, but the police are faster than me. They lunge towards Karen, but she yanks Meg's hair harder backwards and grips the glass more firmly.

'One step further,' she says, 'and I drive this straight through her neck.'

Meg whimpers. Everyone is still for a second, then one of the police officers nods, and they all take a stride back.

'Or perhaps,' Karen says, her tone light, as though she's considering her shopping options, 'I should push it into her heart?' She places the glass dagger against Meg's chest, trailing it idly in a circle. Blood from the tip stains Meg's white T-shirt.

'It's not too late, Karen.' The officer who spoke to me – the one who seemed in charge – speaks to her in a calm, measured voice. 'You can still make the right choice. If you hurt Meg you'll go to prison for a long time.'

Karen's lips tighten. 'I lost my husband and son in one day,' she says. 'I'm already serving a life sentence.' There's a rawness about her tone – about the pain in her eyes – that tugs at my heart. I take a deep breath.

'I'm sorry for your loss.'

'Are you?' Karen spits the words. 'I don't think so. It was too late for Michael, but Jake . . . Jake had a chance. You took that chance away.'

In her head it makes perfect sense, I realise. Jake's heart was giving up. There was a heart waiting for a patient. In Karen's mind, that heart was the difference between life and death. Does that make her mad? Or just mad with grief?

'Jake had other injuries, Karen,' I say carefully. 'Other life-threatening injuries.'

'You took the heart that could have saved him,' Karen says. 'Have you any idea what it feels like to lose a child? For the hand you've held for so many years to be cold to the touch? Do you know what it's like to choose a coffin for your child? To put his favourite songs onto a playlist for a funeral instead of a party?'

The lump in my throat makes it hard to speak. 'It isn't Meg's fault, Karen. Let her go.'

'You can't imagine, can you?' She gives a hollow, bitter laugh. 'But you're going to find out.' She twists the glass again, releasing a fresh trickle of bright red blood. Meg screams, and I spin from one police officer to another.

'Do something! For God's sake do something!'

But it's Meg who does something. Meg who brings one knee up to her stomach, so fast I almost miss it, and then kicks back and upwards, like a donkey. Karen cries out, bending forwards, her free hand on her injured groin, and Meg smashes her head against Karen's.

The glass falls, shattering on the washroom floor, and there's a surge of movement on either side of me, as police rush forward. Meg runs to me and I wrap her in my arms. I smell the sharp, metallic tang of blood, and the sweet scent of my daughter. Safe at last.

They put Meg on a stretcher, wheeling her past the curious eyes of holiday-makers to the ambulance waiting outside. She has stopped crying, but she clings to me, not letting go of my hand as I climb inside to sit next to her.

'She said it was a holiday, Mum,' she sobs. 'She told me you hated me, that you wouldn't care if I was there or not.'

'Shh, sweetheart, it's all okay now.' I call Steve as soon as I can – *it's okay, she's safe, it's all okay* – and he meets us at the hospital, pale and shaking.

'They made an announcement,' he says, hugging me so hard I think I might break. 'Gates closed due to an "incident". I felt so helpless, Lizzie.' He is close to tears.

'It's okay, it's all okay,' I murmur. 'Meg was amazing.' We turn and look at her, and she gives a shaky smile. 'It's just a precaution, the paramedics said. The cuts to her neck look worse than they are. But they're concerned about shock, and with Meg's medical history they need to be extra careful.'

'All that stuff about her son,' Steve says. 'The

way he loved baked beans, and Westerns, and Irn-Bru . . .'

'All lies.'

Looking back, I realise Karen never offered any information about what Jake had liked. Everything was in response to something Meg liked. *Jake loved that too!* Karen would say. And I believed her.

'I hope they throw away the key,' Steve says bitterly.

I didn't see them handcuff Karen. I didn't watch them take her away. The police told us there would be statements to take, and a trial, in due course. But for now I don't even want to think about Karen Edwards. I just want to be with my family.

'How are you feeling, love?' I ask Meg, when she's been moved to a bed, and the nurse has pulled the curtain tight around us.

'Okay,' she says. She gives a wobbly grin. 'It's enough to give you a heart attack, though.'

I don't know if I want to cry or laugh, and I end up doing a bit of both. My baby girl's going to be just fine.

Chapter 13

Moving On

I stamp my feet to warm them up, pushing my gloved hands into my pockets. Mist rises each time I breathe. It's Saturday morning and Meg's playing football. I was reluctant, at first, but the school has been brilliant. The teachers speak regularly with Meg's consultant to make sure she isn't pushed too far. Samira was keen, too.

'The fresh air will do her good,' she said.

Meg's been full time at school for a year, now – playing sport for six months. Her friends look out for her, and slowly – very slowly – I'm learning to let go a little. I still worry when she's late home, or when her mobile is switched off, but I'm getting there. Steve and I are stronger than ever now. I guess we realised how lucky we were, and how much we nearly lost.

The ref blows the whistle for half-time – Meg's team is already two goals up – and I root in my bag for her water bottle. My fingers brush the letter that arrived this morning, with its black stamp across the front: HMP OAKVIEW.

Karen has to have permission to write to me. All prisoners' letters are screened, only sent on to pre-approved addresses. When the prison rang, I wasn't sure. But I gave it some thought, and finally said yes. After all, it was a letter from Karen that started all this – maybe a letter would finish it.

The trial had been fast. Karen entered a guilty plea, meaning Meg and I didn't have to give evidence, and I was grateful she had spared Meg from that.

The first letter came six weeks later. An apology. She's had a lot of time to think – help from prison therapists – and she knows what she did was wrong. *I know how it feels to lose a child*, she wrote. *I wouldn't wish that on anyone else.*

Meg doesn't want anything to do with Karen, and nor does Steve.

'She's insane,' he said, when I showed him the first letter. 'Don't trust a single word she says.'

But her letter moved me, and I wrote back, and so we have become pen pals, of sorts. She tells me about prison life, and asks for my forgiveness. I tell her I'm working on it.

'Heartless cow,' Steve calls her, but I think it's the opposite. A heart big enough to love, big enough to grieve. Big enough to rule her head and stop her thinking straight. She took Meg because she loved Jake so much she was desperate to do something – anything – to take away the pain.

Only it doesn't work like that. The pain we inflict on others doesn't take away our own despair. That is a journey we have to walk alone. Karen was right when she said she started a life sentence the day Jake and his dad died, and now she's serving a prison sentence as well. I wouldn't take that away from her even if I could. She deserves to face justice for what she did, but if I can find it in my heart to forgive her, I will.

Chapter 14

Forgiveness

Dear Karen,

It's strange to think that we are both seeing therapists, in very different places. Mine has an office at the top of a steep staircase above a doctor's surgery. She has shiny leather sofas and boxes of tissues wherever you look. She lets me talk about Meg – not just about what you did, but about before. About when Meg was a toddler, and they found the cancer. About the chemo, and the months in hospital. I told her about Meg getting sick again, about the agonising wait for a transplant. And I realised I've spent the last twelve years waiting for Meg to die. It was bound to affect me, the therapist said.

I think it's all coming out now – all those years of worry, building up inside me. I've stopped my shifts at the chocolate factory. We've had to take out a loan, but we'll cope, we always do. And I've started taking walks, whatever the weather. I see the therapist once a week, and I spend time with Meg and with Steve, and slowly I think I'm getting better. In a funny sort of way I think I needed everything to come to a head. So that I could move on and start seeing Meg as a young woman, not my sick child.

All of which is a very long-winded way of saying: I forgive you. I understand that a mother's love is stronger than anything else in the world. I know how bitterly you regret letting it take over. I forgive you, Karen.

Lizzie.

Karen Edwards reads the letter a second time. She smiles.

Karen isn't seeing a therapist. She gave up after the second session, spending her time instead in the gym or the library – exercising her body and her brain.

But Lizzie bought it. Just like she bought Karen's tear-stained apologies. *Please forgive me, Lizzie, I lost my mind for a while, I'm better now . . .*

Karen didn't lose her mind. She is in full possession of her mind, which tells her what it's told her every day for the last three years. Jake should have had the heart that Meg Thomas had, and with it, he might have lived. With it, she wouldn't be here, in this noisy, filthy prison with inmates who call her names and spit in her food, and hiss *child molester* as she passes them. If Karen blamed Lizzie before, now she blames her two-fold.

She will be out in a few years, if she keeps her nose clean. The Thomas family will be worried, for a while. They'll bolt their doors and check over their shoulders, but gradually they'll realise nothing bad is going to happen.

Or so they'll think.

Because one day, when they least expect it, Karen is going to take what's hers. An eye for an eye; a life for a life.

One day, Karen is going to make Lizzie Thomas pay.

To join the NHS Organ Donor Register, visit organ-donation.nhs.uk or call 0300 123 23 23

THE READING AGENCY

About Quick Reads

"Reading is such an important building block for success"
- Jojo Moyes

Quick Reads are short books written by best-selling authors. They are perfect for regular readers and adults reading for pleasure for the first time. Since 2006, over 4.8 million copies of more than 100 titles have been read!

Available to buy in paperback or ebook and to borrow from your local library.

Turn over to find your next Quick Read...

A special thank you to Jojo Moyes
for her generous donation and support of Quick Reads and to **Here Design**.

Quick Reads is part of The Reading Agency, a national charity tackling life's big challenges through the proven power of reading.

www.readingagency.org.uk
@readingagency   #QuickReads

The Reading Agency Ltd. Registered number: 3904882 (England & Wales)
Registered charity number: 1085443 (England & Wales)
Registered Office: Free Word Centre, 60 Farringdon Road, London, EC1R 3GA
The Reading Agency is supported using public funding by Arts Council England.

Supported using public funding by
**ARTS COUNCIL
ENGLAND**

Find your next Quick Read:
the 2020 series

More from Quick Reads

For a complete list of titles and more information
on the authors and stories visit

www.readingagency.org.uk/quickreads

Continue your reading journey

The Reading Agency is here to help keep you
and your family reading:

Challenge yourself to complete six reads
by taking part in **Reading Ahead**
at your local library, college or workplace
readingahead.org.uk

Join **Reading Groups for Everyone** to find a
reading group and discover new books
readinggroups.org.uk

Celebrate reading on **World Book Night**
every year on 23 April
worldbooknight.org

Read with your family as part of the
Summer Reading Challenge
at your local library
summerreadingchallenge.org.uk

For more information, please visit our website:
readingagency.org.uk

THE SENSATIONAL *SUNDAY TIMES* BESTSELLER
and winner of the Theakston Old Peculier
Crime Novel of the Year 2016

'A terrific, compelling read
with an astonishing twist
that floored me'
PETER JAMES

'Extraordinarily atmospheric,
Mackintosh's emotional
debut doesn't miss a beat'
ALEX MARWOOD

A tragic accident. It all happened so quickly.
She couldn't have prevented it. Could she?

In a split second, Jenna Gray's world descends into
a nightmare. Her only hope of moving on is to walk
away from everything she knows to start afresh.
Desperate to escape, Jenna moves to a remote cottage
on the Welsh coast, but she is haunted by her fears,
her grief and her memories of a cruel November
night that changed her life forever.

Slowly, Jenna begins to glimpse the potential for
happiness in her future. But her past is about to catch up
with her, and the consequences will be devastating . . .

The twisty, gripping number one bestseller,
winner of the RICHARD AND JUDY
SUMMER BOOK CLUB 2017

of urban paranoia'
RUTH WARE

When Zoe Walker sees her photo in the classifieds section
of a London newspaper, she is determined to find out
why it's there. There's no explanation: just a grainy image,
a website address and a phone number. She takes it home to
her family, who are convinced it's just someone who looks
like Zoe. But the next day the advert shows a photo of a
different woman, and another the day after that.

Is it a mistake? A coincidence?
Or is someone keeping track of every move they make . . .